The Reunion

Jacqueline Pearce

ORCA BOOK PUBLISHERS

National Library of Canada Cataloguing in Publication Data
Pearce, Jacqueline, 1962-

The reunion

"An Orca young reader"

ISBN 1-55143-230-7

1. Japanese Canadians--Evacuation and relocation, 1942-1945--
Juvenile fiction. I. Title.

PS8581.E26R48 2002   jC813'.6   C2002-910854-3

PZ7.P302Re 2002

Library of Congress Control Number: 2002109530

Summary: When Rina and Shannon cannot resolve their
differences, Rina's grandmother tells them a tale of lost friendship
from her own childhood, a story set in the small logging town of
Paldi during WWII when Japanese Canadians were interned.

Orca Book Publishers gratefully acknowledges the support of
its publishing programs provided by the following agencies:
the Department of Canadian Heritage, the Canada Council
for the Arts, and the British Columbia Arts Council.

Design by Christine Toller
Cover & interior illustrations by Darcy Novakowski
Printed and bound in Canada

IN CANADA
Orca Book Publishers
PO Box 5626, Station B
Victoria, BC Canada
V8R 6S4

IN THE UNITED STATES
Orca Book Publishers
PO Box 468
Custer, WA USA
98240-0468

04 03 02 • 5 4 3 2 1

For Craig and Danielle

Acknowledgements

I would like to thank Bachese (Bea) James, Chiyoko (Chick) Akiyama and Pat McLean for sharing with me their memories of life in Paldi, and Bea James for lending me many of her old photographs.

I am grateful to Joan Mayo for her book, *Paldi Remembered: 50 years of life in a Vancouver Island logging town*, which was a valuable resource on the history and life of Paldi. Joan also graciously invited my dad and me into her home to talk when we showed up at her Paldi house to ask for directions to where things used to be.

I would like to thank Balinder and Amrik Parmar for help with Punjabi words, Jean-Pierre Antonio and his students for their help with Japanese words, and Donna Baknes and friends for checking my use of Punjabi and Japanese.

Donna, whose parents both lived in Paldi, shared her memories of the Paldi reunion and read an early draft of my story with her daughter, Chloe.

I would also like to thank my dad, Jack Pearce, who drove me out to Paldi and shared his knowledge of logging history and logging communities in the Cowichan area.

Author's Note

The characters and actions in this novel are fictional. However, the town of Paldi is a real place, and the Japanese people really were taken from their homes during World War II.

Paldi grew up around a sawmill built by a man named Mayo Singh in the early 1900s and was named after a village in India where Mayo Singh was born. When Mr. Singh started the sawmill on southern Vancouver Island he invited men who had come from India, Japan and other places to work for him. By 1942, when this story takes place, families of many different cultural backgrounds lived in Paldi, which had both a Sikh temple and a Buddhist temple. In other parts of Canada, many immigrants experienced prejudice. Even in the town of Duncan, down the road from Paldi, some stores would not serve non-whites, and people with different skin colors had to sit in different sections of the town theatre. In Paldi, however, everyone lived, worked, went to school and played together. Many friendships were formed between people of different cultures.

In 1942 Canada was at war with Germany and Japan. Many people feared the Japanese army might attack Canada's west coast, and they worried that anyone who looked Japanese could be a spy. In April 1942 the Canadian government ordered the "evacuation" of all people of Japanese descent (even those born in Canada). These people were removed from their homes to internment camps in the interior of British Columbia. Most lost almost everything they owned. Despite the suffering and hardships, many Japanese people from Paldi kept in contact with their friends back home. Some moved back to the area near Paldi after the war was over. Some met again at the Paldi reunion.

Chapter One

Shannon and Rina

"You brought enough stuff to last a month!" Rina said as she bounced down onto the bed beside Shannon's open suitcase. Her short dark hair swished against the sides of her face.

"Just what I need for a week," Shannon said, laughing. "I hope your little sister doesn't mind lending me her bed."

"Who cares if she does?" Rina said. "I cleared out a drawer for you," she added, pointing to the squat white dresser between the two beds.

"Thanks," Shannon answered. She took a yellow happy-face alarm clock off the top of her clothes and set it on a corner of the dresser, facing her bed. Then, she pulled out a photograph and placed it beside the clock, tucking an edge under the clock's metal base to secure it.

In the picture, the two girls stood with their arms around each other, grinning at the camera. One had short brown hair and a bright smile that shone across her whole face. The other had long blond hair and a shy tilt to her head. Rina had given Shannon the photo at the end of the school year. On the back, Rina had scrawled *friends forever*.

Shannon smiled to herself and thought of the photo she'd given Rina in exchange. On the back of hers, she'd printed neatly *for a purr-fect friend* and drawn a little picture of a cat. Rina had stuck her photo on one side of the mirror that hung above the dresser. Underneath it, she'd taped a cutout of two cartoon cats.

"What's that?" Rina asked, peering

into Shannon's suitcase.

Shannon pulled a bulky object free from the sweatshirt it was wrapped in.

"Roller blades!" Rina exclaimed. "When did you get those?"

"My mom and dad gave them to me a couple days ago."

"What for?"

"Because they're going away, I guess." Shannon looked down at her suitcase. She felt a sudden lump in her throat.

"Wow! Are you ever lucky," Rina said.

Shannon swallowed and shrugged.

"Hey!" Rina said. "My feet are the same size as yours. We could take turns using them. If you don't mind," she added.

"Good idea, but shouldn't I finish putting my stuff away first?"

"Nah. Come on, let's go!" Rina jumped up and tugged Shannon after her.

The summer sun was still high in the sky. Shannon sat down on the grass beside the driveway to pull on the roller blades. She fumbled with the knee and elbow pads, wondering why she didn't feel as excited as Rina seemed to be. She tightened her bicycle helmet and got unsteadily to her feet.

"I'm not very good yet," she said.

"That's okay. You only just got them," Rina told her. "Wait till you see me. I've never tried roller blades before at all."

Shannon smiled. Rina was always good at giving encouragement. Shannon skated jerkily up and down the driveway a few times, then gave up the skates and pads for Rina to try.

At first, Rina was just as shaky on the skates as Shannon — but only for about five minutes. By the time she'd skated down the driveway and back, Rina was gliding like someone who had been roller blading for months.

"Hey, you're doing really great!" Shannon said. She should have known that Rina would be better than she was — even though Shannon had already been practicing on them for two days.

"Can I just go down the driveway one more time?" Rina asked.

Shannon hesitated, then said, "Sure."

One more time turned into another. By the time it was Shannon's turn again, Rina's mother was calling them in for supper.

"Look out!" someone yelled from behind them on the driveway.

Shannon whirled around to see Rina's two older brothers speeding toward them on their bikes.

"Watch it!" Rina called after them, as she and Shannon scrambled out of the way.

The two boys laughed. They jumped off their bikes, dropping them onto the grass, and ran ahead of Rina and Shannon into the house.

"Brothers are so annoying," said Rina as they walked past the bikes, which lay with their tires still spinning. "Sorry you didn't get another turn," she added. "You can go as long as you want after supper."

Once inside, they washed up and headed to the kitchen.

"I got to pick what we're having for supper tonight — in honor of your visit," said Rina. "Guess what it is."

The answer was easy. Shannon knew what Rina's favorite food was.

"Hot dogs!" Shannon said with a grin.

The kitchen smelled of boiling wieners and something else Shannon wasn't sure about. Shannon and Rina squeezed in at one end of the already crowded table. Everyone seemed to be talking at once. Rina's brother, Rob, bumped Shannon's arm as he reached past her for the mustard. Nobody noticed that he didn't say *excuse me* or ask for someone to pass it to him. He squirted the mustard onto his hot dog with a rude noise.

Shannon never would have gotten away with that at her house. Suppers with her parents — just the three of them at a big roomy table — were always quiet and polite.

"Try a samosa," said Rina's grandma, who had joined them for supper and was sitting across from Shannon. She held out a plate of what looked like some kind of fried dumplings. "I made a big batch for the Paldi reunion."

"They're East Indian food," Rina explained. "They have potatoes and peas inside. They're great with ketchup."

Shannon knew that Rina's family background was part East Indian — and part English or Scottish or something, like Shannon's.

"You're supposed to eat samosas with chutney," Rina's mom explained. "But these kids like them with ketchup."

"These kids like everything with ketchup!" Rina's dad teased from the other end of the table.

"That's right!" Rina said, reaching in

front of her little sister to grab the ketchup bottle.

"Hey!" Julie protested, pushing Rina's arm out of her way.

Rina ignored Julie and squeezed ketchup onto her hot dog and her plate. Then she took a samosa in her fingers, dipped it in the ketchup and took a big bite.

Shannon copied Rina. Her teeth sank into hot potatoes, peas and unfamiliar spices.

"It's good," Shannon said politely as the others watched her. Then she felt the heat of the spices growing in her mouth. She grabbed her glass of milk and took a long drink. Everyone at the table laughed.

"It's a good thing I didn't make them hot!" Rina's grandma said, her eyes twinkling.

That night, Shannon and Rina lay on their beds in the warm bedroom, their covers thrown back. Shannon's mind whirled with pictures from the day. Her legs felt like they were still roller blading down

the driveway. After supper, they'd skated even longer, and Shannon had finally felt herself beginning to improve.

"I'm sure glad you're here!" Rina whispered across the space between them.

"Me too!" Shannon whispered back. Then, just for a moment, tears stung the back of her eyes. But that was crazy. She really was happy her parents had let her stay with Rina instead of making her go on the holiday with them. Why wouldn't she be?

Chapter Two

The Fight

Rina's mom took all the kids swimming several times that week. One day, she drove them all the way to Lake Cowichan. They passed through big stretches of forest, which Rina's mom told them had been replanted when she was a girl. They passed areas where the view opened out to low rolling mountains, mostly green, but with some newly logged patches. Partway there, Rina's mom pointed out the turnoff to the small town of Paldi, where Rina's grandma had grown up.

"We go there to the Sikh temple," Julie piped up from the back seat of the van.

"You get to come with us to the Paldi reunion," Rina told Shannon. "It's going to be at the Duncan Forest Museum, so it should be fun."

In between swimming trips, Shannon and Rina roller bladed, walked downtown and hung out at the school playground. They were having a great time, just like they'd expected. It was only when things were quiet at night, and once when Shannon was alone in the bathroom, that she felt that odd feeling in her throat. She told herself that she just wasn't used to the constant noise and activity. At home, it was much quieter, just her and her parents. Here, she never had any time to herself. Once, Rina's brothers had even wrestled their way into the girls' room and onto Shannon's bed. Rina had yelled at them to get out and tried to push them off the bed, while Shannon stood back, well out of their way. She was not used to older brothers.

On the second to last morning, Shannon went back into the bedroom to get something from her drawer. Her clothes were messed up as if someone had been looking through them.

That's strange, Shannon thought. Could Rina's little sister have been looking in her drawer?

When she went outside to where Rina was putting on the roller blades, the striped socks caught her eyes at once.

"Hey, those are my socks!" Shannon said.

Rina looked up, her eyebrows raised in surprise.

"I didn't think you'd mind," she said.

Shannon reddened slightly.

"Well, you could have asked first," she mumbled.

"You were in the washroom," Rina said, shrugging it off.

Shannon didn't say anything more.

"Hey! I have an idea," Rina announced. "You can ride my bike and tow me to the school."

Shannon frowned.

"I'll tow you back," Rina added.

"Okay," Shannon agreed.

Shannon took her time buckling on her bicycle helmet and climbing onto the bike. Rina grabbed hold of the back of the rat trap, and Shannon pushed off. The extra weight made the bike unsteady and pedaling difficult.

"Can't you go any faster?" Rina called from behind.

Shannon pushed harder on the pedals, and gradually the bike picked up speed.

"Ya-hooo!" Rina cheered, letting the sound of her voice stretch out as she flew behind Shannon.

Shannon pedaled hard, grimacing. Finally, Rina let go as they reached the school driveway. They both coasted to a stop in front of the school.

"That was great!" Rina said. "Do you want to try it?"

"No thanks," Shannon grunted. She was

sweating and out of breath. "Let's go to the playground."

"Go ahead if you want," Rina said. "I'll just skate around here a bit first."

Shannon tugged the bike over the curb and pushed it across the grass to the playground. She leaned the bike against a bench, then plunked down onto one of the swings. She stared down at the gravel, tightness creeping into her throat.

The rest of the day did not go much better. All Rina wanted to do was roller blade. After supper, when Rina reached for the roller blades to head back out with them again, Shannon grabbed them first.

"What are you doing?" Rina asked.

"I'm going to put them away for a while," Shannon said.

"What for?"

"They are my skates, aren't they?"

"Yeah, but why can't I use them?"

"You used them all week," Shannon snapped.

"What are you getting so weird about?" Rina snapped back.

"I am not getting weird."

"Well, you're acting pretty strange, then."

"You're the one who's strange. Like you're obsessed or something."

"What are you talking about?" Rina said.

Shannon hesitated for a moment. What *was* she talking about? Why was she getting so upset at Rina? They were supposed to be best friends, but she couldn't seem to stop the words from coming. It just got worse and worse.

By bedtime that night, the girls were not speaking to each other. After the light was turned out, Shannon lay on her bed, staring into the darkness. On all the other nights, they'd stayed awake talking long after they'd gone to bed. Now, she could hear Rina move in the bed just a few feet away, but neither of them said a word. Shannon thought of the photo of her and Rina that lay beside her on the dresser.

Friends forever. For the first time since she'd arrived at Rina's house, Shannon felt alone.

Chapter Three

The Photograph

"You girls seem quiet today," Rina's mom said the next morning as they sat at the kitchen table eating cereal and toast.

"Oh, we're just tired, I guess," Rina answered.

"They had a fight!" Julie chimed in.

"We did not!" Rina hissed at Julie.

Rina's mom looked from Rina to Shannon, her eyebrows raised. Was she going to ask them if what Julie said was true? Shannon looked down. What would she say? That she didn't know what was going on? That she didn't want to stay with Rina any more? Would that be true? A thump at the back door made Shannon jump.

"That must be Grandma," Rina's mom said. "You kids do something for a while, but don't go away. We'll be getting ready to go to the reunion soon."

She opened the door, and Rina's grandma stumbled into the kitchen, her arms piled high with a large cardboard box and two plastic containers of samosas.

"Good morning, everyone!" Rina's grandma said as she set the things down on the kitchen counter.

"What's in the box?" Julie asked, popping up under her grandma's arm. "Is it a present?"

"No, no," Rina's grandma laughed. "It's just old photographs and things."

"Oh," Julie said, her smile disappearing. "I guess I'll go watch TV, then. Bye."

Normally, Rina and Shannon would have exchanged a look over Julie's behavior, but this morning things were different.

"I guess we should go get ready," Rina said, getting up from the table. She headed out of the room without looking at Shannon. Shannon followed her to their bedroom, not sure if Rina wanted her to come. But where else did she have to go?

Shannon tried to look busy, refolding and rearranging her clothes. She wanted to ask Rina what she was going to wear to the reunion, but Rina had her back to Shannon, and Shannon didn't want to be the first to break the silence. She looked back down at her clothes. This was not how she had imagined spending her last morning with Rina. She pulled out a yellow top and matching shorts and put them on. Then she glanced over at Rina.

Their eyes met. They both scowled and looked away.

Shannon sat down on the bed with a sigh and reached to the dresser top for her hairbrush. It wasn't there.

"Where's my brush?" she blurted out.

"I didn't take it, if that's what you think!" Rina snapped.

"Well, I put it right here, and now it's gone. It didn't walk away on its own, did it?"

"Maybe your cooties carried it away!" Rina said.

Shannon was stunned. She stared at Rina until Rina looked away.

At that moment, a muffled giggle came from under Shannon's bed. Rina's head snapped around. She marched over, bent down and flung up the bottom edge of the covers.

"Julie! Get out of there!" she demanded.

Julie wiggled out from under the bed. She was holding Shannon's brush.

"Cooties!" she repeated with a snort of laughter. "Maybe cooties took it!"

Shannon stepped forward and snatched her brush from Julie.

"Hey! You hurt my hand," Julie protested.

"Watch what you're doing," Rina warned.

"I didn't hurt her," Shannon snapped.

"She's just being a brat!"

"Don't call my sister names!"

"Yeah!" Julie said, stretching her body up as tall as she could. "If you're mean, you can't come to the reunion with us."

"Fine!" Shannon said, the words bursting out of her. "I don't want to go. I wish I'd never come to this house at all!"

She glared at Rina. Rina glared back.

"Girls." Rina's grandma stood in the doorway. She looked at them for a moment. "Rina and Shannon, would you come out here for a minute? I want to show you something."

"What about me?" Julie asked.

"You get changed for the reunion," Rina's grandma said. She ushered the other two girls into the living room. Shannon's stomach tightened as she followed Rina.

Rina's grandma sat down on the couch behind a coffee table scattered with old black-and-white photographs. The cardboard box they had come in sat on the floor.

Shannon waited for Rina's grandma to begin a lecture on fighting or at least ask them what was going on. Instead, she reached out and picked up one of the photographs.

"Here's a picture you might find interesting," she said.

"What is it?" Rina asked, sitting down on the couch beside her grandma.

"Come on, dear." Rina's grandma smiled at Shannon and patted the couch seat on her other side. Shannon sat, glad that the older woman was between her and Rina. She took a deep breath and tried to focus on the photograph.

The photo that Rina's grandma was holding showed a group of children standing in front of a wooden building. Underneath the photo was written *Paldi School, 1941*.

"That girl looks like Rina," Shannon said, pointing at a girl in the front row. The girl had the same bright smile as Rina, but her hair was pulled back from her face as if it were long and tied at the back in a ponytail or a braid. Like all the girls, she was wearing a dress — or maybe it was a skirt. Of course, it couldn't be Rina. These pictures were so old.

Rina's grandma smiled.

"That was me," she said. "When I was the same age as you two."

She pointed at another face in the picture. The girl had short dark hair and a shy smile.

"That was my best friend, Mitsu," she said.

"She doesn't look East Indian," Rina commented.

"Oh no." Rina's grandma laughed. "My family came from India. Her family came from Japan. Both our dads worked in the Paldi sawmill."

"I didn't know any Japanese people lived in Paldi," Rina said.

"Oh yes. There were East Indians, Japanese, Chinese, English and others too back then. We all played together."

Shannon wanted to stay back on the couch where she didn't have to look at Rina, but the photographs drew her and she leaned forward.

"What was it like in Paldi?" she asked

"It was a great place for us kids," Rina's grandma said, with a distant smile. "Mitsu and I did all kinds of things together."

"Are you still friends now?" Rina asked.

Rina's grandma's smile faded.

"No," she said softly. "Something happened."

Shannon wondered what it could have been, but she didn't think she should ask. Rina, however, didn't hesitate.

"What?" Rina demanded. "What happened?"

Rina's grandma was quiet for a moment.

"Well, the war was on," she began. "But that wasn't where the trouble started."

Shannon inched a little closer to Rina's

grandma. Out of the corner of her eye, she saw Rina do the same. They settled in to hear the story.

Chapter Four

Jas and Mitsu

It was the beginning of April, 1942. We poured out the front door of the Paldi school, so happy that spring was here. Mitsu and I ran ahead of the others down the wooden steps. I even remember how the air smelled — sweet from new growing things mixed with the tang of fresh-cut cedar, wood smoke and diesel from the sawmill.

I didn't usually pay attention to the smells and sounds of the mill — the steady throb and squeals or the splashes of logs being dumped into the holding pond by the railroad tracks. The sounds were there all the time — except after eleven each night and when there was a holiday or

28

an accident. But everything seemed to stand out that day.

At the bottom of the stairs, Mitsu got ahead of me.

"Race you!" she called.

"Hey, that's cheating!" I complained, but Mitsu didn't stop.

Even though Mitsu was smaller than I was and had shorter legs, she was fast. I had to run hard to catch up. My long braid flew out behind me, and my school bag bumped against my leg. Our feet made a noise like drums on the wooden boardwalk.

I had almost caught Mitsu when my skirt flapped and caught around my knees. I lost my balance.

"Ahh!" I called out as I fell off the boardwalk and landed with a splash in the muddy road.

Mitsu turned back to see if I was all right.

I stood up, mud dripping down my clothes.

Mitsu started to laugh. She laughed so hard that she had to hold onto her stomach.

"It's not funny!" I said, frowning at her. Then I looked down at myself and held up my muddy hands to reach for her.

"I'm a creature from the mud swamp!" I said in a deep monster voice. She squealed and jumped out of my way, and I started laughing, too.

After that, we walked the rest of the way to my house, talking and joking.

"We better go to the back door," I said. "Maybe I can get changed before my mom sees us."

As we stepped inside, Mitsu became shy and quiet. She was always like that around my parents.

"Come on," I whispered.

"Jasminder, is that you?" My mom came into the kitchen. She was wearing a white hand-knit sweater over her blue kameej, which is like a long shirt worn with loose, matching pants called sulwar. She was carrying my baby brother, Nanjo.

"Ah, Mitsu. It is good to see you," she said, smiling. Her English had a heavy East Indian accent.

"Nice to see you, Mrs. Mohan," Mitsu said in a small voice. She dipped her head politely, then looked shyly away.

"Can I go to Mitsu's for supper?" I asked.

My mom looked at me and frowned.

"*Ay key kitta?*" she said, which is Punjabi for "What did you do?" I knew she was mad, because she was forgetting to speak English in front of Mitsu.

"I fell in the road," I explained.

"Go!" She pointed toward my bedroom. "Change those clothes. Then you can help me cut some vegetables."

"Aw, Mata, can't Pritam do it?" Pritam was my older sister.

"She's at the hall, helping with the packages for the Red Cross drive."

"But, Mitsu . . ."

"Help me first. Then you can go to Mitsu's."

Once I had changed into a clean skirt, blouse and sweater, and a pile of carrots and potatoes had been cut, Mitsu and I set out.

We walked along the gray boardwalk past the rows of small wooden houses. Two boys from school ran past us. One of them, Peter, had bright red hair. He flicked my braid as he brushed by.

"Hey!" I shouted. I hated it when he did that. I wanted to chase after them, but Mitsu held my arm.

"Just ignore them," she said.

"Oh, all right." I didn't want them to get away with it, but maybe it would bug them more if we ignored them.

At the end of the street, we turned the corner toward Mitsu's house. Up ahead, the two boys were standing, leaning off the boardwalk over the road. Peter was poking a stick down into the mud, and they didn't look up when we walked by.

"Remember, ignore them," Mitsu said again. Then she leaned past me and gave Peter a push.

He lost his balance and stepped off into the mud.

"Hey! What did you do that for?" Peter shouted, spinning around to face his friend.

"I didn't do it! It was Jas!" said the other boy.

I was so surprised, I didn't say anything.

"Come on!" Mitsu grabbed my sleeve, and we started to run.

"I'll get you Jasminder Mohan!" Peter yelled as he climbed back up to the boardwalk, waving the stick. As we looked back, a big clod of mud dripped off the end of the stick and landed on his jacket. With a whoop of anger, the boys thundered after us down the boardwalk.

We reached Mitsu's house and burst through the front door, gasping for breath. We slammed it shut behind us, leaned against it and began to laugh. The boys' shouts still reached us from the street.

Chapter Five

❧❧❧

Supper

Mitsu and I took off our shoes and left them by the front door, as we always did at Mitsu's house.

"I'm home!" Mitsu called in English, then in Japanese, "*Tadaima kaerimashita*!"

Mitsu's mother came to meet us. She was small and had soft black hair rolled back around her kind, round face. She wore a pale blue dress and had a white lace-edged apron tied around her waist.

"*Okaerinasai*!" she greeted us, smiling. "Welcome home! Welcome, Jasminder!"

"Hello, Mrs. Takashima," I said politely.

"I'm glad you've come to join us,

Jasminder," said Mitsu's mother. "Perhaps you girls would like to help set the table."

We followed her into the kitchen. On the stove, vegetables were frying in a wok, and a pot of fragrant rice was steaming on the back burner. I guessed that a second covered pot contained miso soup. Mitsu's mother went to the stove. Mitsu took five white plates out of the wall cupboard and handed them to me.

"Is Tom going to be here?" I asked as we set the plates onto the blue-and-white tablecloth. Tom was Mitsu's older brother.

"I think so," Mitsu answered. She began placing a matching rice bowl and a pair of chopsticks beside each plate. "Why do you ask?"

"I was just wondering."

"You don't have a crush on him, do you?" Mitsu teased.

"No!" I changed the subject. "Hey, that was a dirty trick you played, you know."

"What trick?"

"On the way here. Pushing Peter so he thought I did it."

"Oh. That was funny, wasn't it?"

"I guess so," I said.

Just then, the front door opened and the house filled with noise and movement as Mitsu's father and Tom came in.

"They flew right over!" Tom was saying. "Three Bolingbroke bombers!"

"They must have been on their way to the base at Pat Bay," Mr. Takashima said.

"All Tom cares about is airplanes," Mitsu whispered.

At supper, we all sat around the table.

"You better get Jasminder a fork," Tom teased. "Or she'll end up with more food on the floor than in her mouth."

I turned red, remembering the mess I'd made at New Year's. In Paldi on New Year's day, all the Japanese families had open house with lots of delicious food set out. Everyone came to visit. When I went with my family to the Takashimas' house, I tried using chopsticks and accidentally dropped several pieces of sushi on the floor.

"Don't be so clumsy!" my mother had hissed.

"It takes time to master anything new," Mr. Takashima was saying kindly. He pushed his round wire glasses back up his nose and winked at me. "I know a certain young man who's been having trouble with his math problems."

It was Tom's turn to redden, and I almost felt sorry for him. I tried to place my fingers around the smooth pointed chopsticks, but they slipped and twisted in my hand.

Mitsu's mother placed a fork beside my plate.

"I think I'll use a fork tonight, too," Mitsu announced. I glanced at her gratefully.

After dinner, Mr. Takashima and Tom moved around the house, pulling heavy black blinds down over all the windows. My father and sister would be doing the same at our house. With the war on, we had a blackout every night so that if any enemy planes flew over, lights would not give away the location of towns.

Mitsu's mother turned the radio on in the living room. An announcer's voice crackled to life.

"Clearing weather unleashed wave after wave of Royal Air Force planes today in their virtually ceaseless offensive against the German-dominated continent."

"An air battle!" Tom said.

"On the Burma front," the deep radio voice continued. "Japanese forces attacked furiously, forcing a further withdrawal of the exhausted British line . . ."

Mr. Takashima sat down in an armchair beside the radio, shaking his head.

"This war is getting worse," he said.

"Shh!" Mitsu's mother said, gesturing toward us.

I met Mitsu's eyes. Grown-ups always thought we were too young to know about the war. But we knew what was happening — at least we thought we did.

"Come on," Mitsu whispered, tugging at my sleeve. "Who cares about the war, anyway?"

We retreated to Mitsu's bedroom. The war was far away, nothing for us to worry about.

Chapter Six

❧

The Gift

Mitsu had a room of her own, though it was smaller than the room I shared with my sister, Pritam. We sat down together on Mitsu's bed, which had a frothy white bedspread covered with tiny pink flowers. The curtains in the window matched. I looked at the shelf beside the bed with its books, the shiny white ceramic cat and the stiff elegant doll that Mitsu's great-grandmother had sent from Japan. As usual, my eyes went to the brand-new Eaton's Beauty Doll with its glossy blond curls and pale blue matching jacket and dress that Mitsu's mother had made for it.

"Can I hold her?" I asked

"Sure."

I picked up the doll and noticed something that hadn't been there the last time I visited Mitsu.

"What's this?" I asked, hooking one finger under the doll's red bead necklace. The beads looked too big for a real doll's necklace. Each one had an orange center, like a small flame.

"I made it," Mitsu said. Then she looked down at the floor.

"It's for you," she said.

"For me? Really?"

Mitsu nodded and reached out to undo the clasp behind the doll's neck.

"It's not really a necklace," she explained. "It's a bracelet."

I put the doll back on its shelf and held out my left hand. Mitsu placed the bracelet around my wrist and did up the clasp.

"It's great!" I said, smiling and moving my arm around so that the bracelet

slid up and down, and the orange at the center of the beads flicked and danced. "I wish I had something to give you."

"You've already given it to me," Mitsu said.

"What?"

"Your friendship."

We grinned at each other. Then Mitsu's mother's face appeared in the doorway.

"Excuse me, girls. Would you like to have a bath? Mitsu's father and Tom have finished. The water is still nice and hot."

"Yes, please!" I said. A bath at Mitsu's was a real treat. At my house, we had to heat water on the kitchen stove, then fill a round steel tub that was set out on the kitchen floor. It was much different at Mitsu's house.

Mrs. Takashima handed us each a bar of soap and a washcloth. Then I followed Mitsu to a door at the back of the house.

"Quick!" Mitsu said as she held open the door. We darted through into the steamy warmth of the bathhouse.

The room was small with a large square wooden bath in the center and benches next to the walls. The bath was heated by a wood fire outside under the room. We took off our clothes and placed them on one of the benches. I laid my bracelet carefully on top of my clothes. We washed and rinsed off using wooden basins that had been set out, then stepped up to the big tub. Mitsu climbed in first, then I lowered myself slowly into the hot steaming water. I sighed happily as the water rose up to my neck. The bath wasn't big enough for swimming, but we splashed and paddled from one corner to another. Soon the water was swirling around like a whirlpool with the two of us caught in the current.

Afterwards, I walked home, fingering the round smooth shape of the beads on my bracelet. My feet echoed hollowly on the boardwalk as I passed the dark houses. Muffled voices and sounds drifted out.

Above the rooftops and the few tall trees that still stood around the village, the sky was a deep purple pricked by tiny points of light. In the distance, the mill hummed and clanked reassuringly. It was hard to believe that, somewhere out there, people were fighting a war.

Chapter Seven

In Trouble

The next day was Saturday. I woke up and saw that Pritam was still asleep in the bed beside me. The house was quiet. My dad would have been up and gone to work hours ago, but where were Mata and Nanjo? I dressed quietly and went out to the kitchen. From the porch at the back of the house came the churning sound of the wringer washing machine and the voices of my mother and little brother. His babyish voice was high and demanding, while my mom's answer was as deep and rhythmic as the washer.

On the kitchen table was a plate of

leftover rotis and a loaf of store bread. I cut myself a slice of bread and spread on a thick layer of blackberry jam, remembering the day at the end of the summer when Mitsu and I and some of the other girls had gone berry picking. We'd hitched a ride on the locomotive engine that took the loggers into the forest each day. The *locie*, as we called it, dropped us off up in the forest outside of camp. We'd picked berries all day, laughing and talking so that the time sped by. That evening, we'd returned home tired, juice-stained and with lard pails full of the small wild blackberries and even some blueberries.

"Oh, good. You're up," my mom said, coming into the kitchen. Nanjo was wiggling in her arms.

"Down, down, down," he cried, reaching for the floor.

"You can watch Nanjo while I hang the clothes on the line," my mom told me as she set Nanjo on the floor.

When she went back out to the porch, Nanjo began to cry, reaching his chubby arms after her.

Sticking the last piece of bread in my mouth, I went to the cupboard, pulled out a big steel pot and a wooden spoon and placed the pot upside down on the floor between Nanjo's legs.

"Watch this, Nanjo," I said, smiling at him and banging the spoon on the pot a few times. He stopped crying at once, grabbed hold of the spoon and began to beat the pot himself.

I sliced myself another piece of bread and spread it with jam, thinking about when Mitsu had found the first blueberry bush. She'd smiled her mischievous smile and thrown the berries up, one at a time, catching them in her mouth as they fell.

I held up my arm and admired the bracelet Mitsu had given me. When I twisted my hand, the beads plunked against each other like berries falling into a pail. What could I give to Mitsu in return? Perhaps my yellow silk chewnee that Mitsu had admired. No, the scarf was new, and my mom would be angry if I gave it away. Maybe I could pick some spring wildflowers. The trilliums and tiger lilies would be out now. I could walk out along the railroad tracks.

"Jasminder!"

I looked up. My mother stood in the doorway, hands on her hips, her face dark.

"Where is Nanjo?" she demanded. "Didn't I ask you to watch him?"

"He's right — " I pointed to the floor, then stopped. Nanjo was nowhere in sight.

"I don't know," I finished. "He was right there a minute ago."

"Well, find him now!" my mother ordered, her voice rising.

I jumped up, and we began searching in cupboards and under chairs.

"How can you be so thoughtless?" my

mother scolded me as we searched. "You can't even watch your own little brother right under your nose."

"I only looked away for a minute," I protested. My mother made it sound like I hadn't been watching him at all. But I was sure I hadn't been distracted that long. I opened a tall cupboard and caught a wooden broom handle as it fell toward me. The metal bathtub crouched on the cupboard floor, but no little boy peered up at me. Where could he be?

"Good morning!" Pritam's cheerful voice broke through the growing panic in the kitchen. She stood in the doorway holding a smiling, dimpled Nanjo.

"Nanjo!" my mother and I cried out.

"He crawled right into my room," Pritam told us. "Isn't he a good boy?"

My mom hurried over to take Nanjo in her arms.

"So, you can crawl now," she cooed, her face pressed up to his. Pritam leaned over to tickle under Nanjo's chin. He giggled.

"What a little man you are," Pritam told him.

My mom and sister both acted as if Nanjo had just done the most wonderful thing. I sighed. At least they seemed to have forgotten about me.

A soft knock on the kitchen door interrupted my thoughts. Mitsu's face peered around the corner. I smiled. Now I'd have an excuse to get away.

"Good morning," Mitsu said in a small polite voice. She held a square tin toward my mother.

"I thought your family might like some rice balls," Mitsu explained. "I helped make them this morning."

My mother beamed.

"How nice!" she said, taking the tin from Mitsu. She turned to me and whispered, "You see how she helps her mother."

I groaned inside. Mitsu's timing was not good.

My mom placed the tin on the kitchen table, and she and Pritam opened the lid to admire the balls of sticky rice inside.

Mitsu moved closer to me.

"Do you want to go to the store with me?" she whispered. "My mom gave me a dime to buy a loaf of bread. That leaves one cent left over for candy."

"That sounds great!" I whispered back.

"You are not going anywhere!" my mother announced, turning her attention back to me. "Not until you help me make pakoras to bring to Mitsu's family."

I opened my mouth to protest, then closed it.

"I guess I'll see you later," I told Mitsu.

"Sorry," Mitsu whispered as she slipped out the door.

Chapter Eight

The Bowl

"That Mitsu is such a nice girl," my mother said as I passed her balls of dough mixed with vegetables to place into the pot of hot oil waiting on the stove.

I wiped my sweaty forehead with my sleeve and tried to blow the loose hair away from my eyes. Why did Mitsu have to bring over rice balls today of all days? My mother thought Mitsu was so perfect. I was tempted to tell her that it was Mitsu who'd played the shoe trick the summer before at the Jor Malla. The Jor Malla was a festival that Mr. Mayo, the saw-mill owner, put on every July. It had games and food, and people came from all around. It always started with readings from the Sikh holy book. When the Sikh people were in the temple with their shoes left out on the porch, Mitsu and Tom had snuck up and mixed up all the shoes. I'd thought it was pretty funny watching everyone try to find the right shoes afterward, but my mother had not.

Finally, three bowls on the kitchen table were filled with golden brown pakoras. I took a pakora in my fingers and blew on it. Then, I popped it into my mouth and savored the spicy mix of potatoes, peas and crispy dough.

"Take this one over to Mitsu's house," my mother directed. She pushed a large brown crockery bowl full of steaming pakoras across the table toward me and placed a cloth over it.

"And don't break the bowl!" she added.

I left the house, grumbling to myself. Of course I wasn't going to break the bowl.

I wasn't that clumsy. My mom didn't seem to care about my feelings any more at all.

At the first corner, I paused to adjust my grip. The bowl was feeling heavier, and my arms were aching. Muffled laughter and footsteps sounded on the boardwalk ahead. I looked up, but couldn't see anyone. It must be some kids playing around the corner, I thought.

What was Mitsu doing right now? I wondered. Had she gone to play with kids at the school field or at someone else's house? I couldn't hear the sound of any kids, but I did hear something. I stopped and listened for a moment. What had I heard? A dog or a cat maybe — under the boardwalk? I walked on again.

Suddenly, one of my ankles caught on something. My foot stopped, but the rest of my body kept going. As I fell forward, the heavy bowl slipped from my fingers and seemed to fly for a moment in slow motion.

"Noooooo!" I cried, reaching after it.

I brought my hands down just in time to stop myself from landing flat on my face. The bowl crashed down in front of me, landing on its side with a terrible cracking sound. The cloth flew off into the muddy road, followed by most of the pakoras.

Stunned, I sat up and stared at the bowl and the pakoras lying in the mud. This couldn't be happening! It couldn't. What was I going to say to my mother? I covered my face with my hands and was about to give in to tears, when I heard something.

I looked back at the spot where my foot had caught. Nothing. Something was odd, though, a shadow of movement between the boards. Then, muffled laughter erupted from right under the boardwalk and two boys rolled out and fumbled to their feet.

"I told you I'd get you, Jasminder Mohan!" Peter said, pointing at me and laughing.

"You . . . you grabbed my foot!" I stammered. I stood up, feeling my face fill with anger. The boys took a step backward. I clenched my fists and stepped toward them. They took another step away.

"What are you going to do, Jas?" Peter taunted.

I moved toward Peter, but he and the other boy turned and ran down the boardwalk.

"You can't get us! You can't get us!" they chanted.

I ran a few steps after them, then stopped. I was never going to catch them now. And what if I did? I closed my fists tighter, digging my fingernails into my palms, and turned back to the cracked bowl, still lying on its side.

"Hey, what's going on?" It was Mitsu. She walked up to me, her eyes taking in the retreating boys and the fallen bowl.

"What happened?" she asked again.

I turned on her.

"This is all your fault!" I said, pointing an accusing finger at her.

Mitsu took a step back. "What do you mean?"

"You're the one who pushed Peter! You're the one who brought the rice balls!"

"But I didn't mean . . ." Mitsu began.

"You think you're so perfect," I went on. My anger tumbled out like water over river rapids, churning and twisting out of control.

"Jas, stop it," Mitsu said. "I'll help you pick things up. It'll be okay."

Mitsu bent down to begin gathering up the scattered pakoras.

Tears stung the back of my eyes. I pushed her away.

"I don't need your help!" I said sharply.

Mitsu stood up and placed her hands on her hips.

"You're supposed to be my friend, Jas," she said matter-of-factly, but there was hurt in her voice. "If you're not going to act like one, I want my bracelet back."

"Fine!" I said. With one sudden movement, I tore the bracelet off my wrist. Too late, I remembered the clasp. The bracelet caught for a moment on the width of my hand. Then it gave. The red beads flew from the broken string, bouncing with tiny plops over the boardwalk and off into the mud.

Mitsu burst into tears, turned and ran.

"Mitsu!" I called. The shock of my own action had stopped the flow of anger with a sudden, sickening bump.

"I'm sorry!" I called after her. But Mitsu was gone.

Chapter Nine

Enemies

The next day was terrible. My mother was as angry about the broken bowl as I'd feared. She called me "clumsy" and "careless" and worse.

My father said he could glue the bowl. But what about my friendship with Mitsu?

On Monday, I walked by Mitsu's house on the way to school, but Mitsu had already left. I could see her and Tom up ahead and considered running to catch up, but what would I say to them? How could I explain? Would Mitsu even listen to me?

The whole day at school, Mitsu and I did not speak to each other. Whenever I looked over at her and our eyes met, she looked away.

At recess a rumor spread through the school that Mounties had driven into Paldi. A boy had seen their police car from the school window. The other kids speculated eagerly about what the Mounties' visit had been about, but I didn't care. I looked across the school field where Mitsu was talking with a group of girls. Was she telling them how rotten I had been? Was she already looking for a new best friend?

After school, I lagged behind the others. I couldn't face Mitsu. My feet dragged along the boardwalk. When I turned the first corner, I could see kids gathering in front of a house. Someone had a ball, so I guessed a game of anti-anti-eye-over was about to begin. By the time I walked up to the house, the kids had divided into two teams.

"Hey Jas!" someone called. "You can be on our side."

I hesitated. Then I saw Mitsu among the group that was moving toward the back of the house. Would I get a chance to talk to her if she played, or would she ignore me?

"Hurry up!" the other kids called.

I waved and jogged over to join them.

"Anti-anti-eye-over!" the boy with the ball called as he flung the ball up over the roof of the house.

The other kids on my team spread out, waiting for the team behind the house to catch the ball and begin running to the front with it. Suddenly, they were coming. Kids were appearing along both sides of the house. I looked from one to another, searching for a sign of the ball. But every one of the returning kids was pretending to hold it. Mitsu ran toward me. Her arms were clutched over her chest as if she was hiding something. Normally, I would have tried to grab her before she could get by, but Mitsu glared at me as if to say, "Don't you dare touch me!" I stood frozen, and she streaked past.

"We made it!" someone called out. The other team cheered, and my side groaned.

"Who had the ball?" I asked a girl.

"Mitsu," the girl said.

My team hurried to the back of the house, but I didn't feel like running. Usually, anti-eye-over was fun, but today my heart wasn't in the game. As I reached the corner of the house, I saw Mitsu's brother, Tom, coming along the boardwalk.

"Mitsu!" he called. "Mom and Dad want you to come home."

"But it's not suppertime yet," she objected.

"This is serious," he said. "They want to talk to us."

"What about?"

Tom glanced around at the rest of us. Finally, he said, "The Mounties came to our house today. They said all the Japanese people have to leave."

"What do you mean?" Mitsu asked, frowning. The other kids around her had stopped to listen.

"It's true," someone else said. "They put signs up on all the Japanese houses."

"It's because Canada and Japan are at war," Tom explained. "The government thinks we might be spies or something."

"Spies?" someone said. Another kid laughed.

"That's crazy!" said Mitsu.

"The Mounties took Dad's camera, our radio and all our maps," Tom went on. "The government thinks we could use them to send information to Japan."

"But why would we do that?" Mitsu said. "We're Canadian, not Japanese."

Tom shrugged. His face was red, and his eyes looked shiny, as if he might cry. I couldn't believe it.

"Just come!" he said, tugging at her sleeve.

Mitsu let herself be pulled away. She

looked as if she thought this was another one of Tom's jokes. I stared after them.

"Hey!" someone called from the back of the house. "What's going on? Are you going to throw the ball or not?"

A face peered around the corner.

"What's taking you so long, Jas? Aren't you playing?"

I watched Mitsu and Tom disappear around the corner along the boardwalk.

"No," I said, turning back to the game. "I think I better go home."

Chapter Ten

Gone!

At supper that night, I told my parents what I'd heard.

"Don't worry," my dad said. "Mr. Mayo will speak to the Mounties. He'll tell them that everyone here can be trusted. No one will be taken away."

At the words "taken away", a heavy feeling crept into my stomach, but my dad's words were reassuring.

Of course the Japanese people in Paldi were not dangerous. The Mounties would see that. Mitsu's mother was born in Canada. Her father had been here since he was a boy. Mitsu and Tom were born here. They were just as Canadian as anyone else.

The next morning I was up early. I got dressed, packed my school bag, wrapped a roti around some cold vegetables to eat on the way, and rushed out of the house. I couldn't wait any longer to apologize to Mitsu. I had to do it this morning. Then everything could get back to normal.

I hurried along the boardwalk. The thud of my feet on the wood planks echoed dully back at me. When I reached Mitsu's house, I slowed down. A white paper was tacked to the front door. The spring breeze lifted it slightly as I walked up to it. *Notice of evacuation*, it said.

I knocked on the door. Would Mitsu listen to me? I waited, but no one answered. I knocked again. A door opened across the street, and I turned to see the mother of one of the kids at school looking at me.

"They're gone," the woman said. "Buses came at six o'clock this morning to take them away." The woman shook her head, as if she couldn't believe her own words. "They're all gone," she said again.

I turned away. I could not believe the woman. What did she mean? Mitsu couldn't be gone. Her family couldn't be gone. I left the porch and rushed around to the side of the house. I stood on tiptoe to peer into the living-room window. The curtains were drawn, and I couldn't see anything. Mitsu's mother always kept her curtains open in the day. Something twisted in my stomach. Panic tightened my chest. I ran around the back to Mitsu's bedroom window. The curtains were open. I stretched to look inside and pressed my face close to the window glass. I could see the inside of the room. There was Mitsu's bed and her dresser, but the bed was bare. So was the dresser. There was no sign of Mitsu anywhere.

I ran the rest of the way to school. Maybe Mitsu would be there. Maybe she'd just left for school early that morning. I would walk into the classroom, and Mitsu would be at her desk. But she wasn't. Half the classroom was empty. All the Japanese kids were gone.

I sat through the school day in a daze. I heard the teacher's explanation, but I still couldn't believe it. The war had seemed so far away. I'd thought it could never touch me. I'd thought I had all the time I needed to say sorry to Mitsu.

After school, I walked past the other kids, not stopping to talk to anyone. The words "gone" and "taken away" floated out at me from the static of voices. I ran, trying to block out the sounds. By the time I reached my house, tears were streaming down my face. I stomped up the back stairs and ran through the kitchen past my mother and little Nanjo. They stared after me.

"Jasminder—" my mother began.

But I didn't stop to listen. I went straight

to my bedroom, flung myself onto my bed and buried my face in the pillow. I heard a sound behind me and knew my mom had come into the room. She was probably going to get mad at me for not taking off my shoes, for running in the house, for not stopping to listen . . . for everything. I kept my face in the pillow and braced myself for my mother's angry words. They didn't come. Instead, I felt a gentle touch on my head.

"Jasminder." My mother spoke softly as she sat down on the edge of the bed. Her hand patted my head.

"*Audhas nah ho*," she said. "Don't be sad."

The unexpected comfort in my mother's voice broke through the wall around me. I felt a twist of pain deep inside, and a loud sob escaped from my throat. How could I not be sad? I rolled over and reached out to my mother — just as I'd done when I was a little girl Nanjo's age. My mother pulled me close and wrapped her arms around me.

As I felt the comfort of my mother's closeness, I promised myself that when Mitsu came back, nothing would stop me from apologizing and making things right between us again.

Chapter Eleven

❦

Repairs

"But Mitsu never came back," said Rina's grandma, ending her story. "I never saw her again."

Shannon and Rina sat stunned and silent for a moment. Then Rina spoke.

"I don't get it? Where did they go?"

Rina's grandma sighed.

"It's hard to explain," she said. "I still find it hard to believe it happened."

She leaned toward the coffee table and pushed aside some photographs, revealing an old, yellowed newspaper clipping. She picked it up and read it out loud.

"*April 21, 1942. On Tuesday morning*

shortly before 10 o'clock all remaining Japanese residents of Cowichan District — 470 of them — left Chemainus on the Princess Adelaide for Vancouver. Of the total, 119 were from Duncan, 104 from Mayo camp and 40 from Hillcrest. Mayo camp is Paldi," Rina's grandma explained. "They were bussed to Chemainus. Then they had to go on an old boat over to Vancouver. Then they were taken to Hastings Park, where the Pacific National Exhibition is now."

"The PNE?" Rina asked. "You mean the fairgrounds? What did they have to go there for?"

"Well," Rina's grandma said slowly. "I guess you could say it was kind of like a prison. Mr. Mayo went to visit the Japanese people from Paldi while they were there. He said there were guards and a fence. All the Japanese people had to live squished into the animal barns. Mitsu's mother wrote to my mother after they left there, but she didn't say much about it."

"Maybe it was too awful," Shannon suggested, her voice small.

"Yeah," Rina agreed, her own voice quieter than usual.

"After Hastings Park they had to go live somewhere in the interior of the province," Rina's grandma continued. "I think it was pretty bad there, too. Then, when the war was over, Mitsu's family moved to Toronto."

"Did you write to Mitsu?" Shannon asked.

"No." Rina's grandma shook her head. "I was never much of a writer."

"Maybe Mitsu will be at the reunion," Rina suggested.

"Maybe," said Rina's grandma. "But if she still lives back east, it would be a long way for her to come."

She stood up slowly.

"Well, I better finish getting ready," she announced. She walked out of the room, leaving Rina and Shannon sitting on the couch with a space between them.

"Wow," Rina said, looking sideways at Shannon. "I never knew any of that stuff."

"Yeah," Shannon agreed.

An awkward silence fell. Roller blades, striped socks or whatever it was that they'd been fighting about suddenly seemed awfully insignificant. What if something had split *them* up before they'd had a chance to make up?

Shannon looked over at Rina, and their eyes met.

"I'm sorry!" they both said at once. Then they laughed.

"I didn't mean what I said about wishing I'd never come here," Shannon said.

"I know," said Rina, twisting toward Shannon. "I didn't mean what I said either."

"I guess I was acting weird because I was feeling sort of homesick," Shannon admitted.

"I should have thought of that," Rina

said. "I should have been nicer."

"Me, too," Shannon said.

"Maybe even best friends need a break from each other sometimes," Rina suggested.

"I guess so," Shannon agreed.

"But not too big of one!" Rina added with a laugh. Then she jumped up from the couch.

"Hey, maybe we should put this stuff away for my grandma," she suggested.

"Sure," Shannon said, leaning forward to push the photos into a pile.

Her eyes were caught by the class photograph with Rina's grandma and Mitsu. Jas and Mitsu. She wished their story hadn't had such a sad ending. She picked up the pile of photos and bent down to place them in the cardboard box. Then she froze.

In the bottom of the box was a red bead.

"Look!" Shannon said. "Do you think that's one of the beads from the broken bracelet?"

Rina dropped to her knees to peer into the box. She plucked out the bead and held it up to the light. An orange flame flickered at its center.

"It must be!" she said.

Rina grabbed the box and set it on the table. She pulled out the few photos and mementos left in the bottom of the box and placed them out of the way.

"There's another one!" she cried, her fingers diving into a corner of the box.

Shannon knelt beside Rina.

"I think there's one stuck under that edge," she said, reaching in.

Together, they pulled out a handful of the small red beads. Then they looked at each other.

"Are you thinking what I'm thinking?" Rina asked, her eyes shining.

Shannon nodded. "Do you have any string?"

"In my room!" Rina jumped to her feet, and the two girls hurried to the bedroom.

Rina pulled a plastic box out from the bottom of her closet, rummaged through it and took out a small pair of scissors, a wound-up length of beading string and a tiny plastic envelope of gold-colored clasps.

"Hey," Shannon said, "I bought you that stuff for your birthday. Haven't you used it yet?"

"No," Rina admitted. "I'm not good at this kind of stuff." She held out the supplies to Shannon. "Maybe you should do it."

"Okay. If you're sure," Shannon said. She was eager to string the beads and see if there were enough to make a bracelet again, but she didn't want to take the job away from Rina if Rina really wanted to do it. After all, they belonged to her grandmother.

"Go ahead," Rina said. "You can do a better job than I can."

Shannon smiled and settled herself on Rina's bed. She placed the beads in a small pile on the bedspread and set to work. Both girls watched as the beads slid one after the other down the string. Would there be enough?

Finally, Shannon held up the completed length of beads. It dangled from her fingers, looking very short.

"Hold out your wrist," she suggested to Rina. "I'll see if it fits before I tie on the clasp."

Rina held out her arm, and Shannon measured the beads around her wrist.

"It fits!" Shannon announced. Her eyes met Rina's, and Rina let out a long breath.

Then Rina frowned slightly. "Now what?" she said.

Shannon shrugged. She'd only thought as far as fixing the bracelet. It had seemed the right thing to do. "I guess we'll just have to see what happens at the reunion," she said.

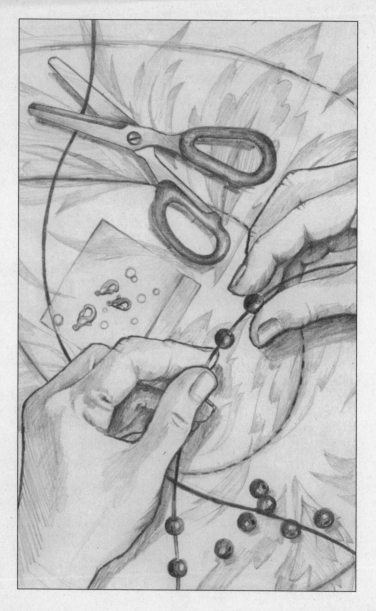

Chapter Twelve

The Reunion

They found Rina's grandma in the kitchen, sprinkling a last touch of paprika on top of an egg salad Rina's mom was bringing to the reunion. Through the kitchen window they could see Rina's brothers doing bike tricks in the driveway as they waited for everyone else to come out. Julie had already claimed the best seat in Rina's parents' van.

"Grandma," Rina said.

"Yes, dear?" Rina's grandma asked, as she stretched plastic wrap over the salad bowl.

Rina held out the bracelet. Rina's grandma

looked up, and the bowl clunked onto the table. Her eyebrows rose and her mouth opened.

"Mitsu's bracelet," she said softly. "After all these years . . ."

She took the bracelet in one hand and held it up to the light. Her eyes got a faraway look. Then they focused again, and she smiled at Rina and Shannon.

"Aren't you sweet. Did you two fix it for me?"

"It was mostly Shannon," Rina said.

"We did it together," Shannon added.

"Well," Rina's grandma said, handing the bracelet back to Rina, "maybe you'd like to keep it now. You could share it."

"But—" Rina began.

Shannon didn't know what to say either. Neither of them had expected Rina's grandma to offer them the bracelet. That wasn't what they'd planned at all.

"Don't you want to give it to Mitsu?" Shannon blurted.

"To Mitsu?" Rina's grandma asked.

"She might be at the reunion," Rina said.

"Ah," Rina's grandma said. "So that's what this is about."

She looked at the girls, her face serious. "I don't want you to be disappointed," she said. "But I don't think Mitsu is going to be there, and even if she is, a lot of years have passed. We may not have anything to say to each other."

She looked at Shannon and Rina's fallen faces and closed her hand over the bracelet again.

"I'll hold onto it for now," she said. "We'll see . . ."

Soon, they were all piling into Rina's parents' van.

When they got to the Forest Museum, they climbed onto one of the open train cars behind a shiny, black, old-fashioned steam engine.

"I think this is the locie that used to come through Paldi when I was a girl," Rina's grandma told them as they settled into their seats.

"What's a locie?" Julie asked.

"It's short for locomotive," Rina answered.

Rina's grandma smiled. "It used to come through Paldi twice a day. The little kids used to run out and wave every time it went by. When I was older, I hitched a ride on it sometimes."

"You hitched a ride?" Julie repeated. "That's funny!"

Shannon and Rina looked at each other. They were remembering the story of how Jas and Mitsu had gotten a ride on the locie when they went to pick berries.

"All aboard!" the conductor called from the platform.

He climbed onto the train, the engineer blew the whistle, and the train headed out of the station. They passed a row of old buildings that had once been used in a logging camp, turned a corner by a wooden lookout tower, then chugged through the center of the museum grounds into the cool shade of trees. They emerged into sunlight again, and the train took them onto a wooden trestle out over the edge of a lake, then back onto land, past an old wooden water tower, and finally to a stop at the station by the picnic area.

As they climbed off the train, they could see a crowd of people already setting out picnic supplies and greeting each other. Draped from the top of the wooden picnic shelter was a banner that read, *Welcome to the Paldi Reunion!*

Julie headed at once for the playground, while Rina's brothers ran to check out some old logging machinery that was on display near the train tracks. Rina and Shannon followed the older people to the picnic area. Rina's mother passed her a red-and-white-checked tablecloth to spread out on an empty picnic table, while she and Rina's grandma began unpacking bags and setting out containers of food.

"Jas Mohan!" Someone came from behind them to greet Rina's grandma. Shannon and Rina turned hopefully. A tall woman with graying blond hair was beaming at Rina's grandma.

"So this is your brood?" she said, sweeping her arms out to indicate all of them.

She was not Mitsu.

People were waving and hugging, laughing and talking all over the picnic area, while kids were running in and out. Some of the people looked East Indian, some looked Japanese, some looked English or European, some looked a mix of everything. Rina's grandma moved around, greeting and talking to different people, but she spoke to each in much the same way. None of them was Mitsu.

"Well, we might as well go and check out the play area," Rina said with a sigh.

They walked away from the picnic area across the grass.

"What's that?" Shannon asked, pointing to a large yellow metal hulk parked on the grass near the play equipment.

"I think it's a caboose," Rina said. "Do you want to see if we can climb onto the top?"

Shannon shrugged and laughed. "All right," she said. "Why not?"

Rina led the way up the caboose steps, then climbed through a wide empty window. She stood outside on the window ledge, reached up and pulled herself onto the roof of the caboose.

"Be careful," Shannon called as she struggled to climb to the window.

A few minutes later, Shannon was sprawled breathless on the caboose roof next to Rina.

"Yuck! It's rusty up here," she said.

Rina laughed. "At least we're away from all the little kids," she said.

Shannon shifted into a sitting position beside her friend.

"Look!" Rina said.

Shannon followed Rina's gaze back to the picnic area.

A new group of people had arrived. Rina's grandma was talking to an older Japanese-looking woman. The woman was small with a round face and short dark hair softened by gray.

Shannon and Rina looked at each other.

"Do you think it's her?" Shannon whispered.

"I don't know."

The two women stood with a slight distance between them. They looked stiff, uncertain.

"I wish we could hear what they're saying," Shannon said, gripping Rina's arm.

"Yeah," Rina said. "Maybe we should go back there."

She twisted her body to begin backing off the caboose.

"Wait!" Shannon said, reaching out to grab Rina. "Look."

Rina stopped and turned back to the picnic area. Her grandma was holding something out to the other woman.

"The bracelet!" Rina hissed.

The woman took the bracelet in her hand. From their distance, it was hard for Shannon and Rina to see her expression at first. Her mouth seemed to drop open slightly as she held the bracelet up to the light. Then, her face broke into the biggest smile Shannon and Rina had ever seen.

It was Mitsu.

The two women embraced. For a moment, Shannon saw the two young girls from the past, Jas and Mitsu — together again, at last.

Quickly, Shannon and Rina climbed down from the caboose and started back across the grass.

"Race you!" Rina challenged, starting to run.

Shannon watched Rina moving easily ahead and away from her. For a moment, she felt a sharp pang in her stomach. Memories of the bad feelings that had passed between her and Rina fluttered back. Then Rina looked back at Shannon, smiled and slowed down. Shannon caught up to her friend, and they jogged up to the picnic site side by side, arm in arm.